This book is dedicated to the all
courageous children everywhere.

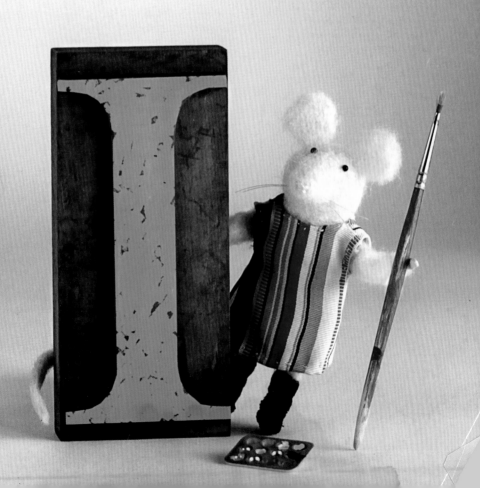

*A Note for Parents and Teachers:*

*Like all **Short Vowel Adventures**,* Princess Pig *highlights one short vowel sound, in this case the short "i" sound. We believe this phonics focus helps beginning readers gain skill and confidence. After the story, we've included two **Story Starters**, just for fun. **Story Starters** are open-ended questions that can be used as a jumping-off place for conversation, storytelling, and imaginative writing.*

*At BraveMouse Books we believe the most important part of any reading program is the shared experience of a good story. We hope you'll enjoy* Princess Pig *with a child you love!*

*The BraveMouse Team*

# Princess Pig

by Molly Coxe

BraveMouse Readers

Brave
Mouse
Books

Pig and Twig
are playing Princess.
"I'll be the princess," says Pig.
"Make three wishes," says Twig.

"I wish for lipstick!"
says Princess Pig.
"Swish! Wish!" says Twig.

"I wish for a picnic!"
says Princess Pig.
"Swish! Wish!" says Twig.

"I wish for a magic trick!"
says Princess Pig.
"Swish! Wish!" says Twig.

"Now I will be the princess,"
says Twig.
"No!" says Princess Pig.
"I wish to make more wishes."

"I wish for nickels!"
says Princess Pig.
"Swish! Wish!" says Twig.

"I wish for pickles!"
says Princess Pig.
"Swish! Wish!" says Twig.

"I wish for popsicles!"
says Princess Pig.
"Swish! Wish!" says Twig.

"Now I will be the princess,"
says Twig.
"No!" says Princess Pig.
"I wish to make more wishes!"

"No more wishes!"
says Twig.
"I quit!"

"I wish to skip,

and sip,

and dip,
with my friend Pig!"

The End

Want to tell a story? Turn the page!

# Story Starters

Twig has a gift for Sis.
What is it?

Pig says,
"Swish! Swish! Make a wish!"
What will you wish?